Girls Love to Burp

For Florence and Grace who have
an expert ability to burp mid sentence

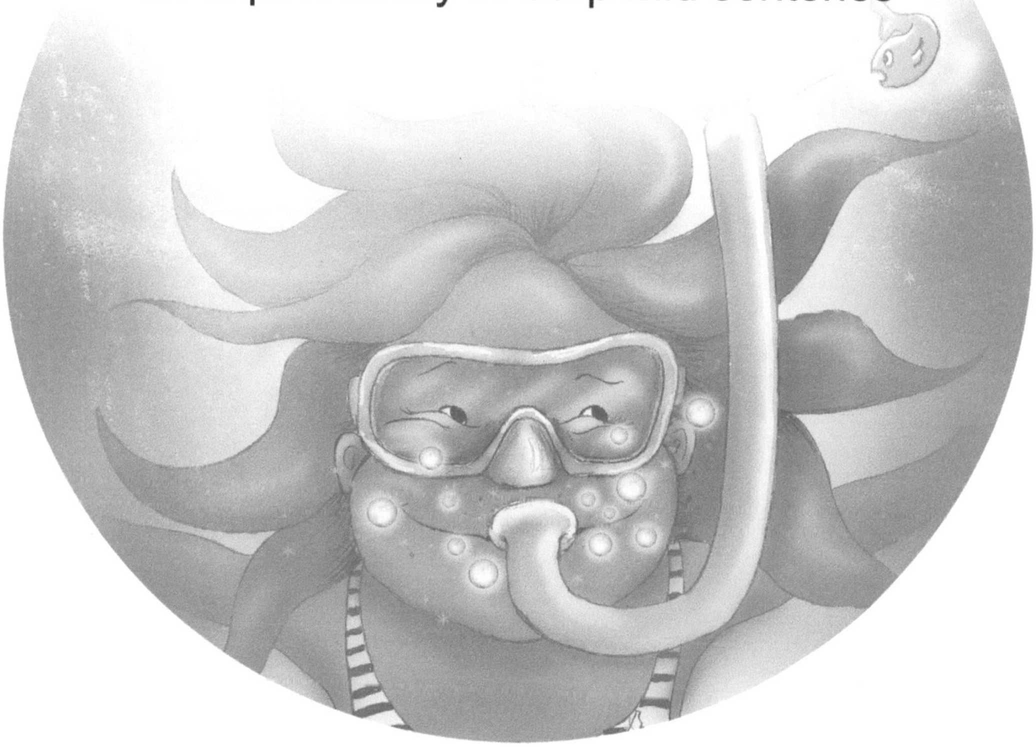

Written by Alice Clover
Illustrated by Cheryl Lucas

Some girls burp in the market
Or snorkelling in the sea

Whilst indulging in delicious cake
And their favourite cup of tea

Some girls' burps are stinky
They may smell like a rotten sprout

Sometimes they blame it on the dog
Which leaves you in no doubt

Girls often burp when they laugh
This makes them burp even more

They love to burp when exploring a cave
So the echo makes rumbles galore

Girls might burp in the morning
When they're steaming in the shower

They burp as they put on their knickers
Knocking over a toiletries tower

Some girls burp as they swing on a rope
And juggle a bunch of balloons

Girls burp as they fly on a dragon
And when they flick peas off of spoons

Sometimes their burps are planned
And other times quite a surprise

They burp after eating a very rich meal
When wearing a subtle disguise

Girls like to burp when they
study
They often feel the need

To burp at their local library
Whilst quietly trying to read
Girls Love to Burp

Some girls burp to their favourite song
Or even when reading aloud

Sometimes they burp with exceptional style
Which makes them excessively proud

Some girls burp eating their ice cream

Or when gulping down fizzy drinks

Their burps might be as loud as a dinosaur

Or as quiet as a mouse that blinks

Girls like to burp
When they play in the sand

Or swing on the monkey bars

Sometimes they burp on a trampoline

Or when driving the bumper cars

They burp playing football with friends
As they dive towards the goal

They also burp as they practice gymnastics
Especially their forward roll

Girls' burps can be explosive
When enjoying a science test

Sometimes they burp being astronauts
Whilst dancing in a vest

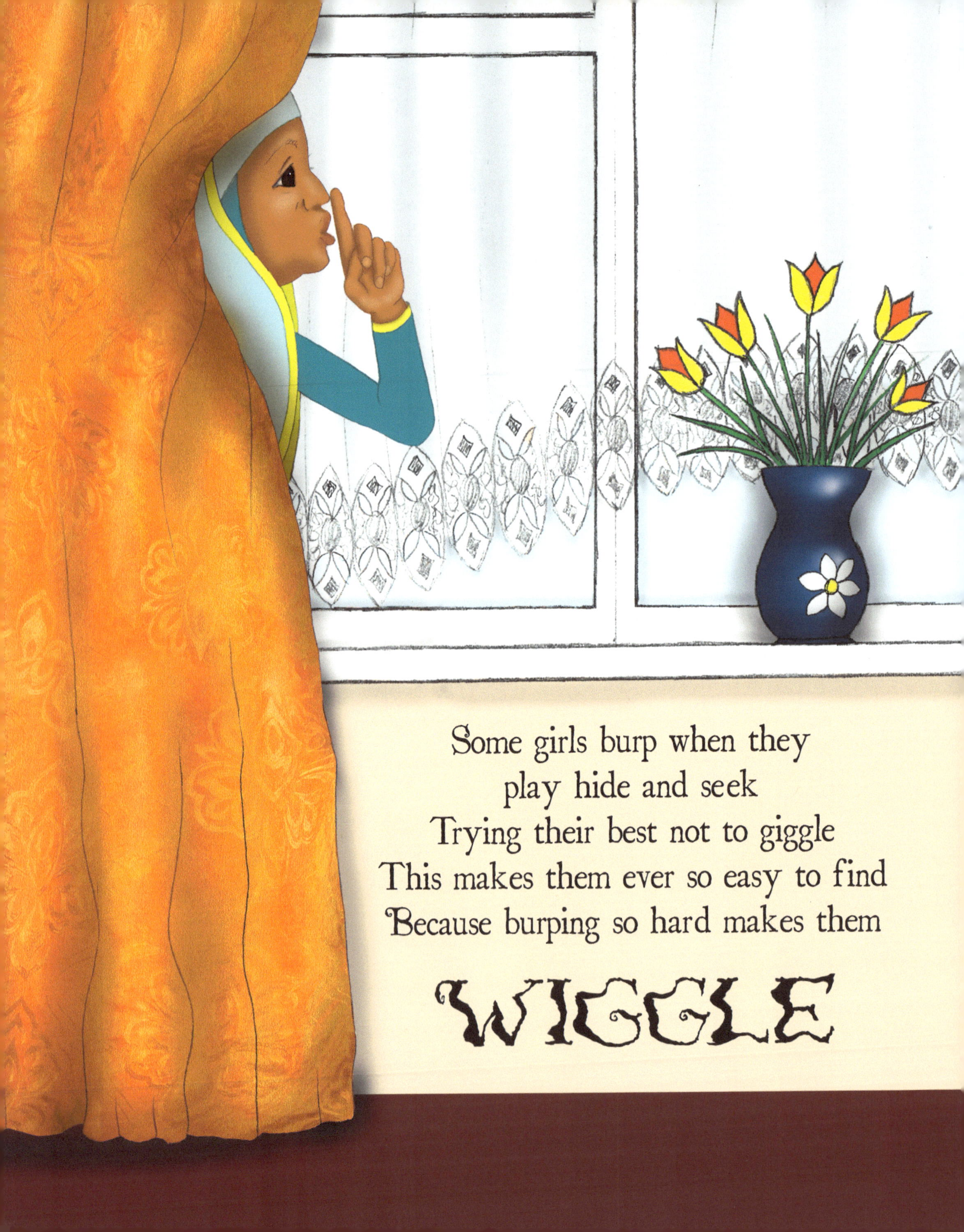

Some girls burp when they
play hide and seek
Trying their best not to giggle
This makes them ever so easy to find
Because burping so hard makes them

WIGGLE

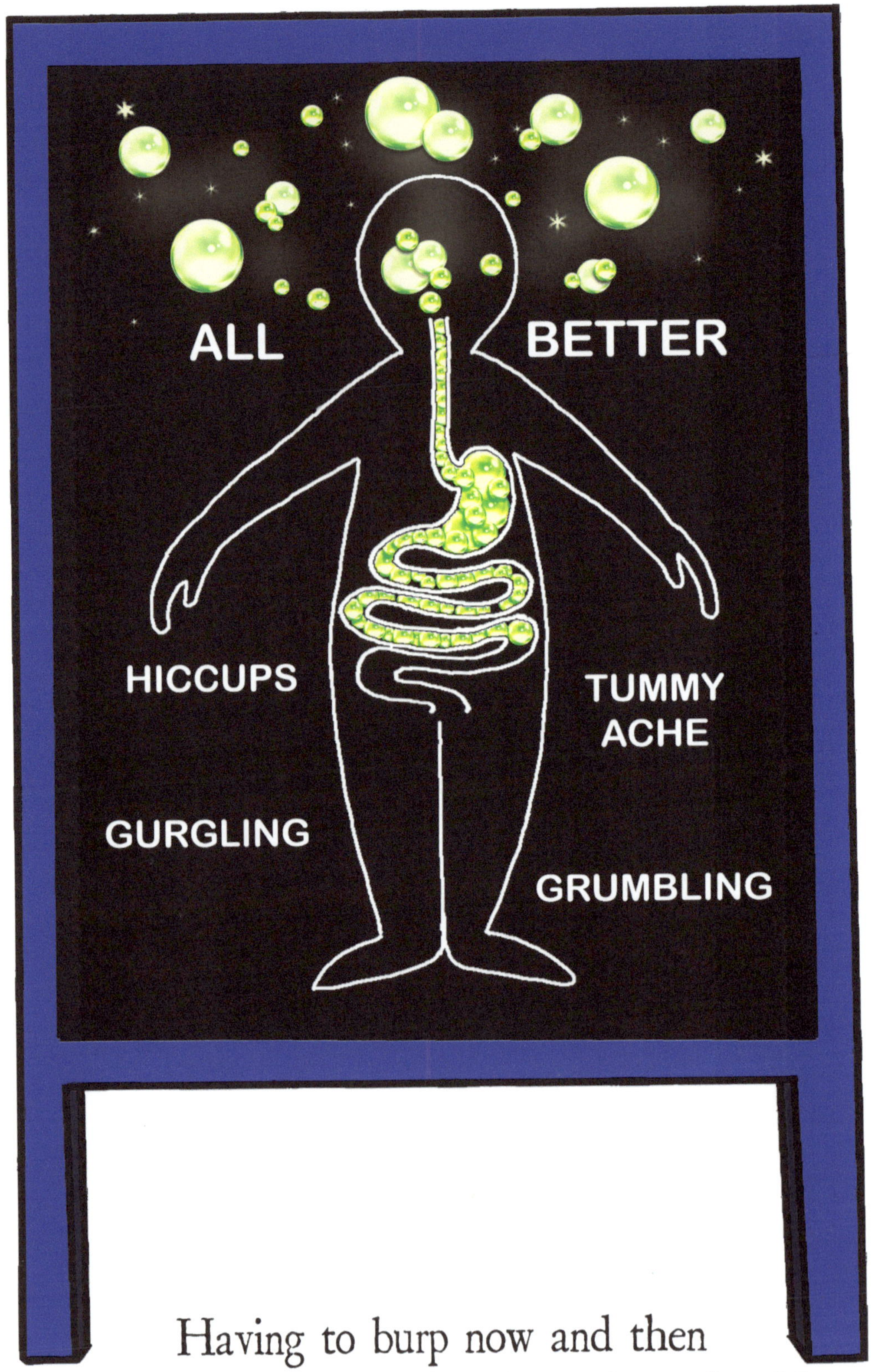

Having to burp now and then
Helps our bodies to work as they should

There is no need to feel ashamed when you do
Because burping can make you feel...

GOOD

Lightning Source UK Ltd.
Milton Keynes UK
UKHW051837181121
394158UK00002B/165